SH

Richmond upon Thames Libraries

Renew online at www.richmond.gov.uk/libraries

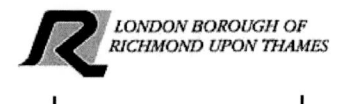

LONDON BOROUGH OF
RICHMOND UPON THAMES

Umbrella

A book to share from

Scallywag Press

FOR OLI AND SYLVIA

Amnesty International UK endorses this book because it celebrates our rights to express ourselves and to choose our own friends

First published in Great Britain in 2019 by Scallywag Press Ltd, 10 Sutherland Row, London SW1V 4JT

Text and illustration copyright © Elena Arevalo Melville, 2019

The rights of Elena Arevalo Melville to be identified as the author and illustrator of this work have been asserted by her in accordance with the Copyright, Designs and Patents Act, 1988.

Designer: Sarah Finan Editor: Janice Thomson

Printed in Malaysia on FSC paper by Tien Wah Press

001

British Library Cataloguing in Publication Data available.

ISBN 978-1-912650-01-9

Umbrella

ELENA AREVALO MELVILLE

Scallywag Press Ltd
LONDON

It was a beautiful morning.

The park would have
been perfect . . .

. . . but Clara had no one to play with.

Then she noticed
the umbrella.

It looked worn but very special.
Clara put it gently on the bench.

THANK YOU!

said the umbrella.

"WOW! You can speak,"
said Clara.

"I can do much more than that," said the umbrella.
"Look inside me. **Anything** is possible!"

And it was true . . .

Here was a **lovely** someone
to play with!

"Thank you, Umbrella!" said Clara.

And who was this coming
down the path?

It was old Mr Roberts from number 44.
He had visited the park for at least two hundred years.

When he was a boy, he thought the park was perfect . . .

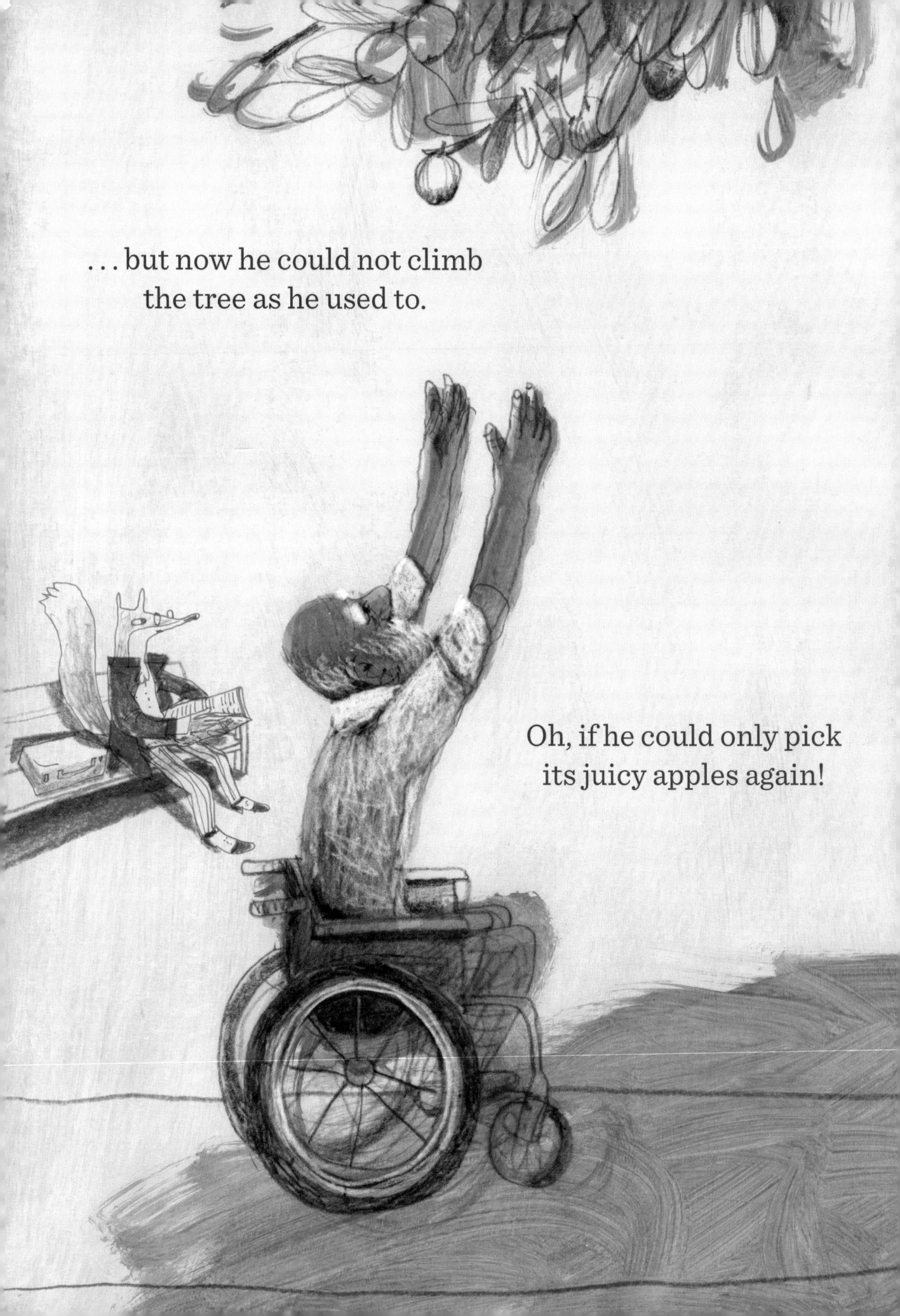

... but now he could not climb
the tree as he used to.

Oh, if he could only pick
its juicy apples again!

"But, Mr Roberts," said Clara, **"anything** is possible."

"Indeed," said the umbrella.
"Look inside me."

An elephant??

"Thank you, Umbrella!"
said Mr Roberts.

And he asked the elephant to pick apples for everyone.

Now the park should
have been perfect.
But whose cries were these?

The Moodies had come out for a picnic
and the boys were having a tantrum.
Everybody was in a bit of a state!

Clara and Mr Roberts knew exactly what to do.

"**Anything** is possible," they said.

"Yes," said the umbrella. "Just look inside me . . ."

A **butterfly** band!

There was **magic** and
music everywhere.

The boys stopped crying.

"Thank you, Umbrella!"

Everyone danced
to the beat
of the band.

Well, not quite
everyone ...

Mr Fox had plans of his own.

"Make me
rich,
rich,
rich!"

he commanded.

But our umbrella does not take kindly to commands . . .

Mr Fox was **drenched!**

Oh dear, WHAT a shower!

A-A-A-CHOO!

sneezed Mr Fox.

BLESS YOU!

said the umbrella.

"Thank you," said Mr Fox.

And suddenly Mr Fox felt ashamed.

He knew **exactly** what to do . . .

"I think this belongs to you," said Mr Fox.

"No," said Clara. "Umbrella belongs
to **ALL** of us."

"Yes, I do," said the umbrella. "Look inside me . . ."

And, right there and then, the park
was absolutely perfect.

Anything is possible.

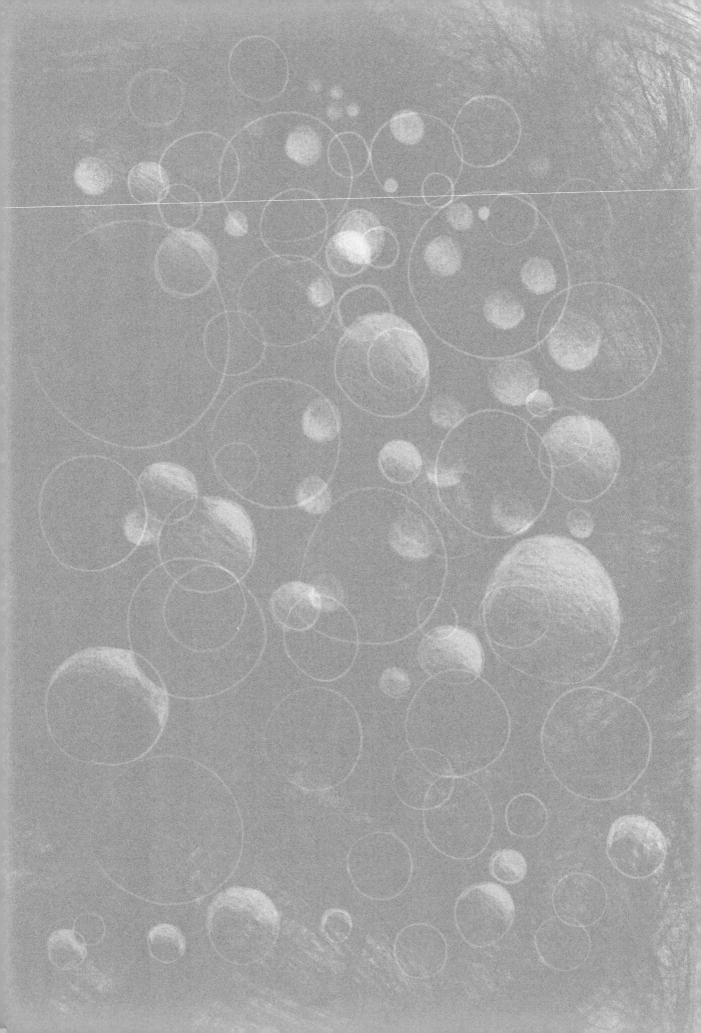